2

Little Whistle's Medicine

CYNTHIA RYLANT

Illustrated by TIM BOWERS

Harcourt, Inc.

San Diego   New York   London

For my friend Eamon
                    —C.R.

To Dr. Anne Littleton and Dr. Vic Ciancetta
                    —T. B.

visit us at www.abdopublishing.com

Reinforced library bound edition published in 2007 by Spotlight, a division of ABDO Publishing Group, Edina, Minnesota. This edition was published by agreement with Harcourt, Inc. www.harcourt.com

Text copyright © 2002 by Cynthia Rylant
Illustrations copyright © 2002 by Tim Bowers

Library of Congress Cataloging-in-Publication Data

Rylant, Cynthia.
    Little Whistle's medicine / Cynthia Rylant ; illustrated by Tim Bowers.
    p. cm.
    Summary: When his friend Soldier hurts his head, Little Whistle tries to find something to make him feel better so he will be able to tell the other toys their bedtime story.
    ISBN-13: 978-1-59961-256-0 (reinforced library bound edition)
    ISBN-10: 1-59961-256-9 (reinforced library bound edition)
    [1. Guinea pigs--Fiction. 2. Toys--Fiction.]   I. Bowers, Tim, ill.
II. Title.

PZ7.R982Lj 2007
[E]--dc22

                                        2006030258

All Spotlight books have reinforced library bindings
and are manufactured in the United States of America.

Little Whistle lived in a wonderful store called Toytown. All day long, he slept in his cage while children brought their parents to look at toys and at him. Some may have thought Little Whistle's life rather dull. But it wasn't at all! For each night, when the shades were drawn, the little guinea pig woke up and set out on a new adventure.

Little Whistle wore a small blue pea coat to keep himself warm as he traveled about the store, visiting all of the toys. The toys were very different when the shades were drawn. They talked and walked and made lovely friends for Little Whistle. He often rode the Toytown train all evening, making stops.

This particular night, Little Whistle had plans to visit Soldier. The little guinea pig was in the mood for a story, and he knew that Soldier read books to the Toytown babies before bedtime. Soldier would have a good story.

But when Little Whistle got off the train at Soldier's toy shelf, things were not well at all. *Soldier* was not well. He lay on his back, holding his head, as all the babies watched him with worry.

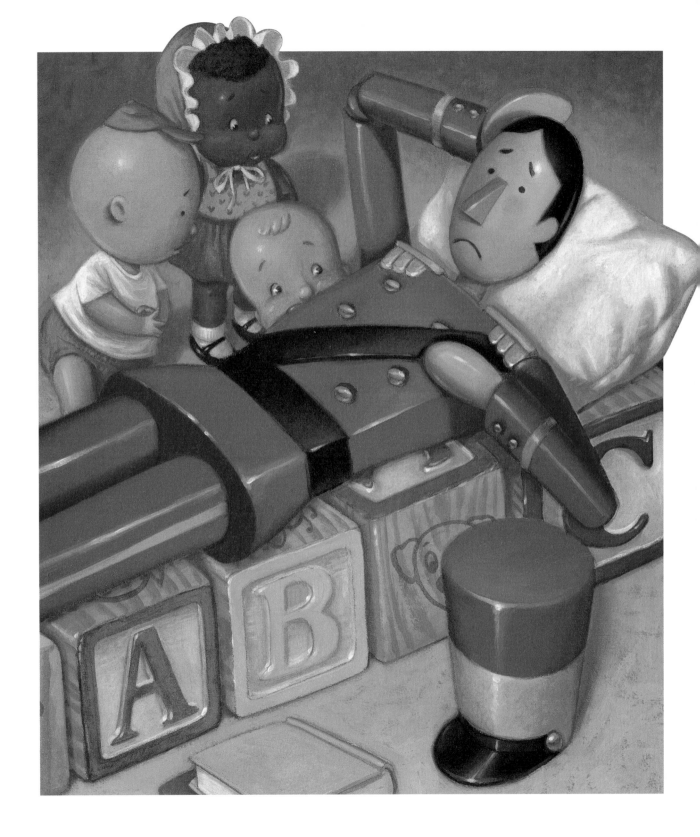

"Soldier, what is wrong?" asked Little Whistle, hurrying to his side.

Soldier groaned.

"Someone bumped me off the shelf today and I landed on my head."

"Poor Soldier!" said Little Whistle.

"I have such a sore head," said Soldier. "I'm afraid I won't be able to read a story tonight."

At this news, all of the Toytown babies began to cry. Big wet tears rolled down their faces.

It was too much for Little Whistle. He did not want the babies to cry. And besides, he had been so looking forward to a story.

"Soldier," the guinea pig said, "there has to be something for sore heads in Toytown. I will find something to make you feel better."

Soldier smiled gratefully and the babies stopped crying. They all watched as Little Whistle boarded the train.

"I'll be back *very soon!*" he called as it pulled away.

He stopped briefly to see his friend Bear, who was wearing a sunbonnet. Bear loved hats.

"Have you anything for sore heads?" asked Little Whistle.

"Would a beret help?" asked Bear, holding up a red one.

"No, thank you," said Little Whistle, and he rode on.

His friend Violet, the china doll, was singing in front of a small white vanity.

"Violet, have you anything for sore heads?" asked Little Whistle.

"Would you like a lullaby?" asked Violet, and began singing one.

But a lullaby could not fix a sore head. Little Whistle thanked Violet and moved on.

His friend Lion had nothing to offer for sore heads except a vanilla cookie. And his friend Rabbit, who ran all around Toytown each night, could not stop herself long enough to listen.

Poor Little Whistle. Poor *Soldier*! Was there nothing in Toytown for sore heads?

But then a kind mother doll who happened to be listening came to Little Whistle's aid. Mothers, of course, always know what to do for sore heads.

The mother doll led Little Whistle to the shelves full of doctor and nurse kits. Little Whistle was delighted! He carried a kit back to Soldier.

The little guinea pig listened to Soldier's heart. He looked inside Soldier's ear. He tapped Soldier's knee. He gave Soldier some medicine and wrapped a bandage round his head.

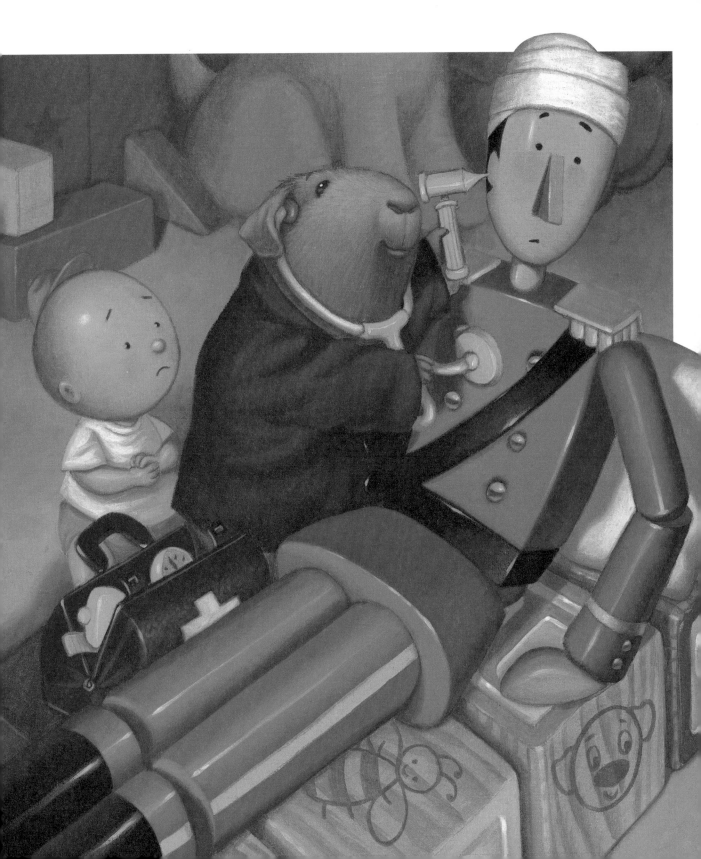

It worked!

"Thank you, Little Whistle," said Soldier with a happy salute.

Then the little guinea pig and all of the babies gathered around Soldier for a story.

And before long…they were fast asleep.

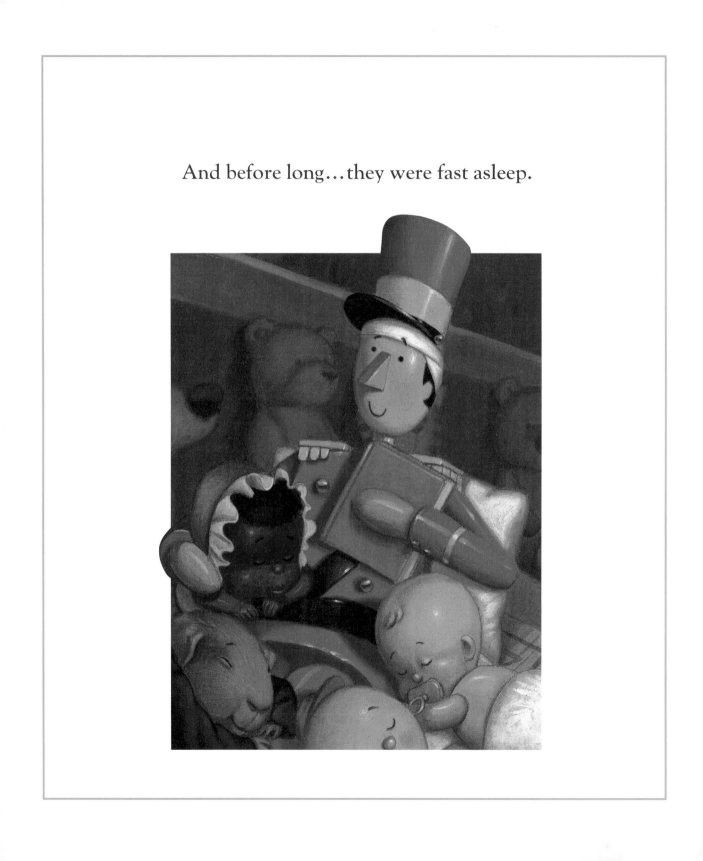